SADDLEBACK *Classics*

THE
Hound of the Baskervilles

ARTHUR CONAN DOYLE

ADAPTED BY

Janice Greene

SADDLEBACK
PUBLISHING · INC.

The Count of Monte Cristo
Gulliver's Travels
The Hound of the Baskervilles
The Jungle Book
The Last of the Mohicans
Oliver Twist
The Prince and the Pauper
The Three Musketeers

Development and Production: Laurel Associates, Inc.
Cover and Interior Art: Black Eagle Productions

SADDLEBACK PUBLISHING, INC.
Three Watson
Irvine, CA 92618-2767

E-Mail: info@sdlback.com
Website: www.sdlback.com

ISBN 1-56254-289-3

Printed in the United States of America
05 04 03 02   9 8 7 6 5 4 3 2 1

CONTENTS

 # Holmes Has a Visitor

Mr. Sherlock Holmes, who usually got up very late in the morning, was sitting at the breakfast table. I was standing in front of the fireplace, looking at a walking stick. A visitor had left it outside our door last night. Engraved on a silver band around the stick were the words: *"To James Mortimer, M.R.C.S., from his friends of the C.C.H."*

Without looking up, Holmes said, "Well, Watson, what do you make of it?"

Holmes was sitting with his back to me. "How did you know what I was doing?" I asked. "I believe you have eyes in the back of your head."

Holmes smiled and said, "This silver-plated coffeepot in front of me makes an excellent mirror. But what do you make of the stick? Since we missed our visitor last night, let me hear what his stick can tell us about him."

"He seems to be an elderly, successful doctor,"

I said. "This handsome gift from his friends shows he is well liked."

"Good!" said Holmes, lighting a cigarette.

"I believe he lives in the country," I went on. "'C.C.H.' is probably a hunting club. I would also guess he walks a great deal. This stick has been very much knocked about."

"*Excellent!*" said Holmes. "Since you have been so kind as to write accounts of my detective work, you should have given yourself more credit. I owe much to you."

Holmes had never given me such praise before. I was pleased indeed.

He took the stick from my hands and examined it with a magnifying glass. "Interesting," he said.

"Has anything escaped me?" I asked.

"I am afraid, my dear Watson, that most of your ideas were wrong. However, the man *is* a country doctor. But I believe this gift came to him from a hospital, not a club. 'C.C.H.' is probably Charing Cross Hospital."

"You may be right," I said.

Holmes said, "It seems likely. I would guess the stick was presented when our doctor left the hospital to start his own practice. He is absent-minded—or he would not have left the stick at our door—and he has a medium-sized dog."

I laughed. Holmes leaned back and blew wispy rings of smoke at the ceiling.

I took my medical directory from the shelf and looked up the name. James Mortimer had indeed worked at Charing Cross Hospital before moving to Devonshire. I showed this listing to Holmes, who smiled in satisfaction.

"No mention of a hunting club," said Holmes, "but he is a country doctor, as you guessed."

"Why do you believe he has a medium-sized dog?" I asked.

Holmes rose and stood by the window. "The tooth marks on the stick are too far apart for a terrier's jaw, and not broad enough for a mastiff. It may have been . . . yes, by Jove, it *was* a spaniel."

"But my dear fellow, how can you possibly be so sure?" I chuckled.

"For the very simple reason that I see the dog himself at our doorstep," said Holmes.

Just then the doorbell rang and Dr. Mortimer entered. He was very tall and thin, with a long nose like a beak. Two big gray eyes sparkled from behind a pair of glasses. When he saw the stick in Holmes'

hand, he ran toward it. "You have it! I would not lose that stick for the world," he cried.

"A gift, I see," said Holmes.

"Yes, sir."

"From Charing Cross Hospital?"

"Yes," said Dr. Mortimer, "it was given to me when I got married."

"Dear, dear, that's bad!" said Holmes, shaking his head.

"Why is that bad?" asked Dr. Mortimer.

"Only that you have upset our little deductions," said Holmes. "You say you got married?"

"Yes," said Dr. Mortimer. "That's why I left the hospital."

"Aha!" cried Holmes. "Then we are not so wrong after all."

"I have wanted to meet you for some time," said Dr. Mortimer. "I have heard that you are the second most renowned expert in Europe—"

"Indeed, sir!" said Holmes sharply. "May I ask who has the honor of being the *first*?"

"To the scientific mind," Dr. Mortimer said, "Monsieur Bertillon would be the first."

Annoyed, Holmes snapped coldly, "Then perhaps you had better go to *him*."

"I said to the *scientific* mind," Dr. Mortimer repeated with emphasis. "But as a *practical* man, you, of course, stand alone. I hope I have not—"

"Just a little," Holmes admitted. "I think, Dr. Mortimer, that you should now tell me the exact nature of your problem."

2 Dr. Mortimer's Story

"I have in my pocket a manuscript dated 1742," Dr. Mortimer explained. "It was given to me by Sir Charles Baskerville. I was his friend as well as his personal doctor. Sir Charles died very suddenly three months ago. He was a strong-minded man, sir. He had as little imagination as I do. Yet he took this manuscript very seriously. It has to do with a legend which runs in the Baskerville family."

Looking confused, Holmes said, "But you wanted to see me about something more *modern*—is that correct?"

"Most modern," said Dr. Mortimer. "This matter must be decided within the next twenty-four hours. It has to do with this manuscript. It was written by Hugo Baskerville to his sons Rodger and John. With your permission, I will read it."

In a high, cracking voice, Dr. Mortimer said, "In 1649, the Manor of Baskerville was held by a young man who was also named Hugo. It must be said that *this* Hugo was a wild, godless fellow.

"Hugo came to love the daughter of a farmer. Fearing his evil name, she would have nothing to do with him. So it came to pass that one night, when the girl's father and brother were away, Hugo and his friends stole down to the farm and carried her off. They brought her to the Hall and placed her—*imprisoned* her, actually—in an upper room. Then Hugo and his friends gathered downstairs for a wild evening of food and drink.

"The poor lass probably had her wits turned with the wild singing and swearing she heard from below. At last, pure fear must have driven her to escape. She climbed down the ivy on the west wall. Then she ran across the moor toward her home.

"Some little time later, Hugo went upstairs to find the cage empty and the bird escaped. He was in a fury. He called to his grooms to saddle his horse and set loose his hounds. He gave the dogs the girl's handkerchief to sniff, and they set off in full cry over the moor with Hugo close behind. Thirteen of his wicked friends followed after him.

"After a few miles, the hunting party stopped cold. They saw Hugo's black mare running wild, her

saddle empty. They rode on slowly until they came to a deep dip in the land. At the head of the dip were Hugo's dogs, gathered together, whimpering.

"Three of Hugo's friends—the boldest, or perhaps the most drunken—rode down into the dip. In the moonlight they saw the maiden lying on the ground, *dead*—no doubt from fear and exhaustion. Close by lay the body of Hugo Baskerville. A great black beast stood over him, tearing out his throat. The thing was shaped like a hound—but larger than any hound the eye has ever seen! As it turned its blazing eyes toward the three men, they ran away, screaming. It is said that one of Hugo's friends died that night. The other two were broken men for the rest of their days.

"This is the tale, my sons, of the coming of the hound. It has cursed our family ever since. I heard the story from my father, who had heard it from his. And it is true that many of our family have died strangely. I beg you both to put your trust in God, and never cross the moor at night, when the powers of evil are strongest."

Then Dr. Mortimer finished reading and turned to Mr. Sherlock Holmes, who yawned.

"Did you not find the manuscript interesting?" Dr. Mortimer asked anxiously.

"To a collector of fairy tales," said Holmes.

Dr. Mortimer took out a folded newspaper article from his pocket. "Now, Mr. Holmes," he said, "this is a newspaper article from May of this year. Let me read it to you."

"*The sudden death of Sir Charles Baskerville has brought sadness throughout the county. Sir Charles, as is well known, made large sums of money in South Africa. When he returned to England, he was determined that the countryside should benefit from his good fortune. His kindness*

13

and generosity were well known.

"'The facts of Sir Charles' death are unusual, but there is no reason to suspect foul play. His doctor, James Mortimer, said that Sir Charles was suffering from ill health. His longtime butler and housekeeper, a married couple named Barrymore, also stated that Sir Charles' health had been failing.

"'The night of his death, Sir Charles walked down the famous yew alley of Baskerville Hall. He had a habit of doing this every night before going to bed. At the same time, Barrymore was indoors preparing Sir Charles' luggage for a journey to London the next morning.

"'At midnight, Sir Charles had not returned. Barrymore became worried and went searching for his master. Because the day had been wet, Sir Charles' footprints were easily traced down the alley. Halfway down this walk there is a gate which leads out to the moor. The footprints showed that Sir Charles had stood at the gate for some time and then had walked away on his toes!

"'A horse dealer, who was on the moor at the time, says he heard cries—but was not sure where they came from. Also, the horse dealer confessed, he had been drinking that evening.

"'There were no signs of violence upon Sir Charles' body, although his face was incredibly distorted. Dr. Mortimer says this is common in the case of heart attack. Indeed, the coroner has ruled that heart attack was the cause of death. This is fortunate indeed—for it puts to rest the wild rumors of Sir Charles' end. If these whisperings had gone on, it might have been difficult to find someone to live in Baskerville Hall and carry on Sir Charles' good work.

"'It is understood that Sir Charles' next of kin is Mr. Henry Baskerville, a nephew. The young man, who lives in North America, will inherit all of Sir Charles' land and fortune.'"

Dr. Mortimer refolded the paper and put it in his pocket.

"Thank you," said Holmes. "But these are only the *public* facts of Sir Charles' death. Now let me have the private ones."

"What I am about to tell you, I have not told anyone," Dr. Mortimer said nervously. "I did not want to add to the many rumors already surrounding Baskerville Hall. But I will be perfectly frank with you.

"I saw a great deal of Sir Charles Baskerville. Besides Mr. Frankland and Mr. Stapleton, the naturalist, there are no men of education for many miles around the hall.

"In the last few months, it became clear that Sir Charles' nerves had become strained to the breaking point. The poor man had taken the legend of the hound very seriously. He never set a foot on the moor at night. Sometimes he would ask me if I had ever heard the baying of a hound.

"About three weeks before he died, we were standing at his door when a look of dreadful horror came over his face. I turned around just in time to see something passing at the head of the drive. It looked like a large black calf. I hurried to the spot where the animal had been. By that time, however, the creature had disappeared.

"The night of Sir Charles' death, Barrymore sent for me. I examined the body and the area in which it was found. It seems that Barrymore had made a strange statement when he gave evidence. He said there were no footprints other than Sir Charles' in the area. But I found some—fresh and clear."

"A man's or a woman's?" Holmes asked.

Dr. Mortimer's voice sank almost to a whisper as he said, "Mr. Holmes, they were the footprints of a gigantic hound."

3 A Mysterious Message

I shuddered at Dr. Mortimer's words. "You *saw* the footprints yourself?" Holmes demanded.

"As clearly as I see you."

"Were there any marks near the gate leading to the moor?"

"No," said Dr. Mortimer. "But Sir Charles must have stood there five or ten minutes. The ash had dropped twice from his cigar."

"*Excellent*!" said Holmes. "Watson, this is a man after our own heart. Were there any other marks or prints anywhere at all?"

"I could find no others."

"If only I had been there!" Holmes cried. "Now all the evidence has been smudged by rain. Oh, Dr. Mortimer—you should have called me sooner!"

"But I *could* not," said Dr. Mortimer, "not without alarming everyone. Besides . . . in some matters, even a great detective is helpless."

"What?" Holmes exclaimed. "Are you suggesting the thing is *supernatural?*"

Dr. Mortimer blushed. "Several times before Sir Charles' death, people reported seeing the hound on the moor. They all agreed the creature was huge and ghostly. Some said it glowed in the dark!"

"You are a trained man of science," Holmes scolded. "Do *you* believe this thing is supernatural?"

"I do not know what to believe."

"If this thing is supernatural," Holmes sneered, "why do you come to me at all?"

"I need your advice," said Dr. Mortimer. "Sir Henry arrives at Waterloo Station in exactly an hour and a quarter."

"Is he the only heir?" Holmes asked.

"Yes," said Dr. Mortimer. "Sir Charles had two brothers. One of them was Sir Henry's father, who died several years ago. The other brother was Rodger, the black sheep of the family. He looked very much like Hugo. When he ran into trouble in England, he left for South America. He died there of yellow fever in 1876. Sir Henry is the last of the Baskervilles. So now, Mr. Holmes—what do you suggest I do with him?"

Holmes said, "I suggest you bring Sir Henry to

call on me tomorrow morning at ten o'clock."

"Yes, indeed, I will do that, Mr. Holmes," Dr. Mortimer said gratefully. He scribbled the time on his shirt cuff and quickly hurried away.

After Dr. Mortimer left, it was clear that Holmes wanted to be alone to think about the case. When I returned that evening, the room was thick with tobacco smoke. Holmes was studying a map.

He said, "Here is the town of Grimpen, where Dr. Mortimer lives, and here is Lafter Hall, the home of Mr. Frankland. Here also is the home of Stapleton. Fourteen miles away is the great prison of Princetown. All around these few points there is nothing but the moor."

"It must be a wild place," I agreed.

Holmes nodded. "It seems odd that Sir Charles spent so much time in front of the gate leading to the moor. After all, the moor was a place he usually avoided at night. And what do you make of the change in his footprints?"

"Mortimer said he walked on tiptoe."

"No," said Holmes. "He was running—running until he burst his heart and fell dead on his face. He must have been crazed with fear. Only a man who had lost his wits would run *away* from the house. This case begins to make sense, Watson. But let us think no more about it until our meeting with Dr. Mortimer and Sir Henry in the morning."

The next day, the clock was striking 10 when Dr. Mortimer and Sir Henry appeared. The latter man was small, dark-eyed, and very strongly built.

Sir Henry said, "This is strange, indeed, Mr. Holmes. On the very morning of our appointment, something quite puzzling has happened."

He laid a long white envelope on the table. It was addressed to Sir Henry Baskerville, Northumberland Hotel.

"Who knew that you were going to that hotel?" Holmes asked.

"No one could have known," Sir Henry said. "We only decided after I met Dr. Mortimer."

Holmes said, "Hmmm. Someone seems to be very interested in your movements." He drew a paper from the envelope. On the paper had been pasted cut-out words that read: *If you value your life, stay away from the moor.* Only the word "moor" had been hand-printed in ink.

"Do you have yesterday's *London Times*, Watson?" Holmes inquired.

"I believe so—yes. Here it is."

Holmes quickly looked over the pages. Then he read aloud: *"You may suppose your business will grow with one of these laws. But in the long run, they will prevent wealth from coming into our country. The value of our goods will drop. And if this happens, our way of life will suffer."*

Sir Henry looked confused. "It seems we've got a bit off the trail here," he said.

"Not at all," Holmes insisted. "Do you see how the words in the letter were taken from this article? *you, keep, value, life.* . . They're all there—except, of course, for the word 'moor,' which it seems was too difficult to find."

"By thunder, you're right!" Sir Henry exclaimed.

"But how did you know to look in the *Times*?" asked Dr. Mortimer.

"No London paper but the *Times* uses this type," said Holmes. "Have you noticed anyone watching you or following you, Sir Henry?"

"Why in thunder should anyone do that?" Sir Henry cried.

"We are coming to that," Holmes replied. "Has anything else unusual happened to you?"

"Well, this will sound foolish—but it seems I've lost one of my boots," Sir Henry complained.

"Oh, I'm sure it will turn up soon," said Dr. Mortimer. "What's the use of troubling Mr. Holmes with such a small matter as your boots?"

"Well, he asked if there was anything unusual," Sir Henry said defensively.

"*Exactly*," said Holmes, "however foolish the matter may seem. Tell me what happened."

"I put the boots outside my hotel room last night to be cleaned. This morning there was only one boot there. The worst of it is, I only bought this pair of boots last night!"

Holmes frowned. "If they were new, then why

did you want them to be cleaned?"

"It was a trifling matter, really. I wanted a darker polish put on."

"I believe the boot will turn up soon," Holmes said reassuringly.

"And now, gentlemen," Sir Henry said firmly. "Please tell me what all this is about."

Holmes smiled. "Of course. Dr. Mortimer, could you please tell Sir Henry the story? Tell it just as you told it to Watson and me."

Dr. Mortimer explained the entire case to the baronet. When he finished, Sir Henry shook his head. "I have heard the story of the hound, but I never took it seriously. But as to my uncle's death—well, it all seems to be boiling up in my head just now. I can't get it clear yet."

"The question now is whether or not you should go to Baskerville Hall," Holmes said.

"Well, my answer is fixed," Sir Henry replied. "There is no devil in hell who can keep me from going to the home of my own people." His face turned red as he went on, "Meanwhile, I want time to think over everything you have told me. Suppose we meet again for lunch at two."

Holmes nodded. "You may expect us," he said.

Sir Henry and Dr. Mortimer decided to walk to their hotel. As soon as the door closed behind them, Holmes cried, "Quick, Watson, we mustn't lose them. Get your hat and boots!"

As we started down Regent Street, we could see Sir Henry and Dr. Mortimer walking about 200 yards ahead.

"Shall I run and stop them?" I asked.

"Not for the world," Holmes whispered.

When the men stopped to look in a shop window, Holmes' quick eyes darted across the way. A hansom cab had pulled up on the other side of the street.

"*There's our man*, Watson!" Holmes exclaimed. "Come along!"

At that instant I saw a pair of piercing eyes and a bushy black beard in the window of the cab. Then I heard the man yell to the driver, and the cab flew off down the street. Holmes ran a few steps after it, but the cab was already out of sight.

Panting in frustration, Holmes came back. "Watson," he said, "if you are an honest man, you will record this failure against my successes!"

Holmes had, however, gotten the number of the cab—No. 2704. We went to the district office, where the manager promised to look it up. Then Holmes sent for one of the manager's boys, a bright lad of 14 named Cartwright.

Holmes handed Cartwright 23 shiny shillings and showed him the hotel directory. "There are twenty-three hotels in this neighborhood," he said. "You will give each hotel porter a shilling to look through yesterday's wastepaper. You will tell the porter that an important telegram has been lost. But what you are *really* looking for is a page of the *Times* with holes cut in it. Do you understand?"

"Yes, sir," said Cartwright.

Holmes told Cartwright to report to him by wire before evening. Then he decided that we should visit some picture galleries nearby. That would fill the time before we were due at the hotel.

4 Sir Henry's Missing Boot

When we arrived back at the hotel, we found Sir Henry standing at the top of the stairs. His face was red with anger, and he was waving a dusty boot in his hand.

"It seems they are playing me for a fool in this hotel," Sir Henry snorted. "By thunder, Mr. Holmes, if these fools can't find my missing boot, they will rue the day they lost it!"

"But surely you said that you were missing a new brown boot."

"Yes," Sir Henry complained, "and now they've taken one of my black ones."

A worried-looking waiter appeared. "I'm sorry, sir," he said apologetically. "I've asked all over the hotel, but no one seems to have your boot."

"Well, that boot had jolly well better be back before sundown, or I'm moving out of this hotel!" Sir Henry cried. Then, turning to Holmes, he said,

"Please excuse me, sir. I hadn't meant to trouble you with such a small matter."

"Not at all. I think it's well worth troubling about," Holmes said.

"Why, you look very serious over it."

"I don't really understand it yet," Holmes said. "This case of yours is very complicated, Sir Henry. But we hold several threads in our hands. The odds are good that one of them will lead us to the truth."

Nothing more was said about the case until lunch was over. Then Holmes asked Sir Henry what he had decided.

"To go to Baskerville Hall," Sir Henry replied.

"On the whole, I think that is the wise thing to do," Holmes agreed. "I have evidence that you have been followed in London. But of the millions of people in this city, it is difficult to discover just *who* is following you. Did you know, Dr. Mortimer, that *you* were followed after leaving my house?"

Dr. Mortimer was startled. "*Followed!* By whom?" he demanded.

"Unfortunately, I don't know just yet," Holmes admitted. "Do any of your neighbors have a full black beard?"

Dr. Mortimer said, "No—or, let me see—why,

yes! Barrymore, Sir Charles' butler, has a dark beard. He is in charge of the hall."

"We should see if he is really there," Holmes said. "We'll send a telegraph to Mr. Barrymore, asking if everything is ready for Sir Henry. Then we'll send a second wire to the postmaster of Grimpen. It will say that the telegram to Mr. Barrymore must be delivered into his own hand."

Dr. Mortimer shook his head in dismay. "Barrymore and his wife *seem* to be a very respectable couple," he said.

"Did Barrymore profit from Sir Charles' will?" Holmes inquired.

"Yes. He and his wife had five hundred pounds each," the doctor answered.

"That is very interesting," Holmes replied.

"I hope that you do not look with suspicion on *everyone* who received something from Sir Charles," Dr. Mortimer said. "I also had a thousand pounds left to me."

"Indeed!" said Holmes. "And how much was the total estate of Sir Charles?"

"It was close to a million."

Holmes raised his eyebrows. "I had no idea such a gigantic sum was involved," he said. "A man might well play a desperate game for such an amount of money. Forgive me for making an unfortunate suggestion—but is anyone named to inherit the estate if you died, Sir Henry?"

"Yes," Sir Henry said. "Since Sir Charles' younger brother Rodger died a widower, the estate would go to James Desmond. He is a distant cousin—a minister, and a very saintly man. As far as I know, he would inherit the money. That is, unless it had been willed to someone else."

"Have *you* made *your* will, Sir Henry?"

"No, Mr. Holmes. I've had no time. It was only yesterday I learned how matters stood."

"Quite so," Holmes acknowledged. "Well, Sir Henry, I believe you should go to Baskerville Hall as soon as possible. But not alone."

"Dr. Mortimer will go with me."

"But Dr. Mortimer has his practice to tend to," Holmes said. "His house is miles away from yours. I would go myself—but I have a case of blackmail I must see to here. No, you must take a trusty man who will always be at your side. I've got it! There is no man better worth having when you are in a tight place than Dr. Watson."

I was completely taken by surprise. Before I had

time to object, Baskerville shook my hand.

"Well, now, that would be very kind of you, Dr. Watson," he said warmly.

The promise of adventure has always fascinated me. And I must admit that I was pleased at Holmes' words of praise.

"I will come with pleasure," I said.

"You must report very carefully to me," Holmes ordered. "When a crisis comes, I will let you know what to do."

We had just gotten up to leave the hotel when Baskerville gave a cry of triumph. Diving into one of the corners of the room, he pulled a brown boot out from under a cabinet.

"*My missing boot!*" he cried.

"This is very strange," said Dr. Mortimer. "I searched this room carefully before lunch."

"And so did I," said Sir Henry. "I searched every inch of it."

We could not make any sense of this. We now had a line of strange events all within two days. These included the printed letter, the black-bearded spy, the loss of the new brown boot, the loss of the old black boot, and now the return of the new brown boot. On the way home Holmes sat lost in silence, deep in thought.

Just before dinner, two telegrams arrived. The first ran as follows:

> *Have just heard that Barrymore is at the hall.*
> *Baskerville.*

The second one said:

> *Visited twenty-three hotels, but sorry to report could not find cut sheet of the Times.*
> *Cartwright.*

Holmes looked disappointed. "There go two of my threads, Watson. But at the same time, there is nothing more interesting than a case where everything goes against you."

"We still have the cabman who drove the spy," I reminded him.

Just then the doorbell rang. It was the cabman himself, a rough-looking fellow.

"I've driven this cab for seven years and never had a problem," the cabman snarled. "I've come to ask you to your face what you have against me."

Holmes smiled. "I have nothing in the world

against you, my good man. In fact, I have some money for you—if you will give me a clear answer to my question."

Now confused but grinning, the cabman said, "Well, this is a good day after all and no mistake. Very well, then. What do you want to know, sir?"

"Tell me all about the man who followed two gentlemen down Regent Street this afternoon," Holmes demanded.

"The truth is," said the cabman, "the gentleman told me that he was a famous detective. His name was Sherlock Holmes."

For a moment, Holmes sat in silent amazement. Then he burst out laughing.

"What a *touch*, Watson!" Holmes cried. "The man has a fine touch, indeed!"

Holmes paid the cabman and quickly wished him goodnight. Then he turned to me with a sad smile. "So *snap* goes our third thread! I've been checkmated in London. I can only wish you better luck in Grimpen. But I'm not easy in my mind about sending you, old boy. It's an ugly, dangerous business, Watson. I shall be very glad when you are back home safe and sound."

5 Welcome to Baskerville Hall

Driving to the train station the next day, Holmes gave me some last words of advice. "I wish you simply to report facts, Watson," he said, "and leave the theories to me."

"What sort of facts?" I asked.

"Anything at all about the case," Holmes said, "especially anything about Sir Henry's neighbors."

"Shouldn't we get rid of the Barrymore couple in the first place?" I asked.

"By no means!" Holmes cried. "If they are innocent, it would be cruel. If they are guilty, we would lose any chance of finding them out. No, we will leave them on our list of suspects. Let's go over them now. There is a groom at the hall, if I remember right. There is Dr. Mortimer, whom I believe is completely honest, and there is his wife, whom we know nothing about. There is this naturalist, Stapleton, and there is his sister, who is supposed to be quite beautiful. There is Mr. Frankland of Lafter Hall, and there are a few other neighbors. *These* are the folk who must be your very special study."

"I will do my best," I promised.

"Keep your revolver with you night and day, and never relax your guard," Holmes advised.

The journey to Grimpen was pleasant. Sir Henry was delighted to see the land he had known as a young man. "Dr. Watson, I've been over a good part of the world, but I've never seen a place to compare with this!" he exclaimed.

To me, the countryside looked very bleak and sad. The moor ahead was empty and gray, dotted with lonely, jagged hills.

Soon the train stopped at a small station. I was surprised to see two soldiers waiting there. They seemed to be watching the road.

A servant from the hall was waiting with a carriage. Dr. Mortimer asked him, "What is this, Perkins? What's going on?"

Perkins said, "They're looking for Selden, sir, the Notting Hill murderer. He escaped from Princetown three days ago. They're watching every road and every station for him."

As the carriage swept over the moor, a cold wind seemed to go right through us. I shuddered. Somewhere out there a murderer was hiding like a wild beast, his heart full of hate.

At last we came to the gates of Baskerville Hall and turned down a dark tunnel of trees. Sir Henry glanced around with a frown. "No wonder my uncle felt troubled about this gloomy place. Why, I'll have a row of electric lamps put up here. In six months, you won't recognize it."

As we reached the house, a tall man with a black beard stepped from the shadow of the porch. He called out, "Welcome, Sir Henry! Welcome to Baskerville Hall!" It was Barrymore, the butler.

Dr. Mortimer said goodbye and drove home, while Sir Henry and I turned into the hall. We were led into a fine, large room and quickly warmed ourselves by the fire.

"Would you wish dinner to be served at once, sir?" Barrymore asked.

"Is it ready?"

"In a very few minutes, sir. You will find hot water in your rooms. My wife and I will be happy, Sir Henry, to stay at the hall until you have found new servants."

"*New* servants?" Sir Henry asked.

"Sir Charles led a very quiet life," Barrymore explained. "Surely you will want to have more company, and more servants."

"But your family has been with us for several generations," Sir Henry protested. "I would be sorry to begin my life here by breaking an old family connection."

Barrymore looked unhappy. "I feel that also, sir—and so does my wife. But to tell the truth, sir, we were very much attached to Sir Charles. His death was quite a blow to us. I fear we shall never again be easy in our minds at Baskerville Hall."

"But where will you go?"

"I have no doubt, sir, that we shall be able to start some kind of small business," Barrymore replied. "Sir Charles' kindness has given us the means to do so. And now, sir, perhaps I should show you to your rooms."

We ate dinner in a long, dark room. Portraits of the Baskervilles, staring down on us as we ate, lined the walls. It was a relief when the meal was over.

I was tired that night, but could not sleep. The house was deathly silent except for a chiming clock. Then suddenly, in the very dead of the night, I heard a sound—the sob of a woman. For an hour I sat up and listened—but heard nothing more.

The next morning, I asked Sir Henry about the sobbing. He had heard it, too. He rang for Barrymore. The man's face seemed to turn pale when Sir Henry asked him about it.

"There are only two women in this house, Sir Henry," Barrymore said. "One is the maid, who sleeps in the other wing. The other is my wife—and I know the sound did not come from her."

At first, I believed him. But after breakfast, I met Mrs. Barrymore. She was large woman with a stern looking mouth. But her eyes were red and swollen. Why had Barrymore lied? And why had the poor woman felt such sorrow last night?

Sir Henry had many papers to look over after breakfast. I took a walk to the Grimpen post office, to ask about Holmes' telegram. James, the postmaster's son, said that he had delivered it.

"Did you put it into Mr. Barrymore's own hands?" I asked.

"No, sir," said the boy. "He was up in the loft at the time, so I gave it to Mrs. Barrymore."

In spite of Holmes' cleverness, we had no real proof that Barrymore had not been in London. It seemed that an invisible net was being drawn around young Sir Henry. It made me very uneasy. As I walked down the lonely, gray road back to Baskerville Hall, I prayed that Holmes would be free to join me soon.

6 Watson Meets the Stapletons

Suddenly, I heard running feet on the road behind me and then a voice calling out my name. It was a small, stiff-faced blond man, somewhere between 30 and 40 years of age. He carried a butterfly net and a tin box for collecting specimens.

It was Stapleton of Merripit House. "How did you know me?" I asked.

"I was with Mortimer," Stapleton explained. "He told me who you were. I hope Sir Henry had a pleasant journey."

"Yes, thank you," I replied politely.

"After the sad death of Sir Charles," Stapleton went on, "we were all afraid that no one would come to live in the hall. I suppose Sir Henry is the sort of fellow who has no fears of that hound that is said to haunt the moor. A number of people here would *swear* they have seen the beast on the moor! Poor Sir Charles was one of them. I have no doubt that that was what led to his sad death."

"But *how*?" I inquired.

"Sir Charles' nerves were quite worked up, you see. Perhaps the sight of *any* dog was too much for his weak heart."

"So you think that a dog ran after Sir Charles—that he actually died of fright?" I asked.

"Have you a better answer?" Stapleton said.

"At this point, I have no answer at all."

"Has Mr. Sherlock Holmes?" asked Stapleton.

The words took away my breath.

Stapleton smiled. "Of course we have heard about you and Mr. Holmes, Dr. Watson. If *you* are here—then Sherlock Holmes must surely be interested in this matter. Will he be coming soon?"

"There are other cases that keep him busy in London," I answered curtly.

"A pity!" said Stapleton.

We had come to a fork in the road. Stapleton invited me to Merripit House to meet his sister. My first thought was that I should be at Sir Henry's side. But then I remembered the pile of papers on his desk and accepted the invitation.

"The moor is a wonderful place, full of secrets," Stapleton said. "I have only lived here two years, but I know it well. Do you see that great plain over there, with the bright green spots on it?"

"Yes," I said.

"It is called the great Grimpen Mire. Just one false step in that dreadful marsh means death to man or beast. Look! By George, there is one of those unfortunate moor ponies right now!"

The vague shape of a large brown creature was rolling and tossing in the mire. Then the pony's neck shot upward, and a horrible cry rang out over the moor. It turned my blood cold, but Stapleton seemed to have stronger nerves than mine.

"The pony's gone," he said flatly. "The mire has him. It's a bad place, the mire. Only one or two paths lead through it. I have found them out."

"But why would you—or anyone—wish to go into so horrible a place?"

"You see the hills beyond the mire?" Stapleton pointed out. "That is where the rarest plants and butterflies are—if you can reach them."

"Perhaps I shall try my luck some day," I said.

"For God's sake, put such an idea out of your mind!" cried Stapleton. "There would not be the *least chance* of your coming back alive! It is only by remembering certain landmarks that *I* am able to go there safely myself."

"*Listen!*" I cried. "What is that sound?"

A long, low moan swept over the moor. The sound seemed to fill the air.

Stapleton had a strange look on his face. "People around here say it is the Hound of the Baskervilles."

"Why, that is the weirdest, strangest thing that I have ever heard!" I cried.

"The moor is a strange place, indeed," said Stapleton. "Look at the hillside over there. What do you make of those?"

I saw that the whole hillside was covered with gray, circular rings of stone. There were at least 20 of them.

I was stumped. "What are they? Sheep pens?"

"No, they are the homes of prehistoric man. Oh, excuse me, sir! That is surely a Cyclopides."

A small moth had flown across our path. In an instant, Stapleton was rushing off after it. To my horror, the moth flew straight for the mire and Stapleton charged after it. Stapleton followed in a zigzag path, looking a bit like a huge moth himself. I held my breath, thinking that at any moment he might slip and be sucked into the mire.

Just then I heard footsteps behind me, and a woman appeared. I had no doubt that this was Miss Stapleton. She was beautiful indeed! There could not have been a greater contrast between brother and sister. While Stapleton had blond hair and gray eyes, her eyes were dark and her hair was almost black. She was slim, elegant, and tall. With her perfect figure and elegant clothes, Miss Stapleton was a strange sight on the desolate moor.

I raised my hat and was about to speak to her when she cried out, "*Go back!* Go straight back to London!"

I stared at her in stupid surprise. "Wh-why should I go back?" I stuttered.

"I cannot explain. But you must leave this place at all cost! Hush now, my brother is coming. Would you mind getting that orchid for me over there? We are rich in orchids on the moor, though it is rather late in the year."

Stapleton walked up to us, breathing hard. "Hello, Beryl," he said in a rather cool tone.

She said, "Well, Jack, you look very hot."

"Yes, I was chasing a Cyclopides. What a pity I missed him." His small, light eyes darted questioningly between me and the girl. "Ah, I see that the two of you have already met."

"Yes, she said. "I was just telling Sir Henry that it is rather late in the year to truly appreciate the beauty of the moor."

"Oh, no," I said, "I am not Sir Henry. I am his friend, Dr. Watson."

Her face turned red. "Oh! Then I have been mistaken," she said nervously. "But will you come, Dr. Watson, and see Merripit House?"

A short walk brought us to the house. The large rooms were elegant indeed. As I looked out the window at the gray, rocky moor, I thought about the Stapletons. I wondered what had brought this well-educated man and this beautiful woman to such a lonely place.

Stapleton seemed to read my thoughts. "A queer spot to choose, isn't it, Watson? Yet we manage to make ourselves fairly happy here—don't we, Beryl?"

"Quite happy," she said. But she did not sound as if she really meant it.

"I had a school," said Stapleton, "in the north country. Shaping the young minds of those boys was very dear to me. But the fates were against us. An epidemic broke out and three of the boys died. I ran out of money and had to close the school. I miss the boys—but the moor is a perfect spot for my studies. Would you like to come upstairs and see my collection of *Lepidoptera?*"

Saying that I was eager to get back to Sir Henry, I said goodbye and set off toward the hall.

I had not gone far when Miss Stapleton caught up with me, her breath coming quickly. "Dr. Watson, I wanted to say how sorry I am about my stupid mistake. Please forget the words I said, which have nothing to do with you."

"Please tell me why you were so eager for Sir Henry to return to London," I said.

"You know the story of the hound?" she asked.

"I do not believe in such nonsense."

"But I *do*," she insisted. "If you can, Dr. Watson, you must take Sir Henry away from this place of danger as soon as possible."

"If this is all you wished to tell me," I said, "why did you seem so worried about your brother overhearing you?"

"My brother is very anxious to have someone living at the hall. Who else will help the poor people of the moor?" She looked around anxiously. "He would be very angry if he knew what I had told you. I must leave now. Goodbye!"

The Barrymores' Secret

From this point on, dear reader, I will follow the events of this most unusual case from my own letters to Mr. Sherlock Holmes.

MY DEAR HOLMES:

So far, I trust that my letters have kept you up to date as to all that has been happening in this lonely part of the world.

We have had no more news of the escaped criminal, who has been missing for two weeks. Since there is no food to be found on the moor, we believe he must have left the area.

As for Sir Henry, it seems he has become very interested in our neighbor, Miss Stapleton. If I am not mistaken, she is strongly attracted to him also. This is no great surprise, for she is a fascinating and beautiful woman. There is something almost *tropical* about her, which makes quite a contrast to her cool brother. There is a dry glitter in his eyes and a firm set to his lips which goes with a harsh nature. You would find him an interesting study.

One would think that Stapleton would welcome a match between Sir Henry and his sister. Yet several times Stapleton has prevented them from being alone. He seems to have a great deal of control over her.

There is one other neighbor I have met since I wrote last. This is Mr. Frankland of Lafter Hall. He is an elderly man, red-faced and white-haired. His passion is law, and he has spent much of his fortune in court. It seems clear that he fights for the pleasure of fighting and can happily take up either side of a question. Apart from the law, he seems to be a kindly, good-natured fellow.

Frankland's other love is astronomy. He has a large telescope. Lately, he's had it pointed at the moor, hoping to spot the escaped convict.

My most important news, however, is about the Barrymores. When we questioned Barrymore about receiving the telegram, he said he was up in the loft at the time it was delivered. Later, however, Barrymore brought up the subject again. He asked Sir Henry if he had done anything to lose his trust. Sir Henry told him that this was not the case at all.

To show his good will, he gave Barrymore several of his old suits.

For my part, I have had my doubts about Barrymore's character. Last night's adventures seemed to bring my suspicions to a head. About two o'clock in the morning, I woke and heard steps passing my room. I got out of bed and saw Barrymore moving quietly down the hallway. I followed him to the end of the hall and peered around the corner. Barrymore was at the window, holding a candle up to the glass. For several minutes he stood watching. Then he gave a deep groan and put out the light. Instantly, I made my way back to my room and soon heard him pass down the hall again. What this all means I cannot guess—but I mean to get to the bottom of it.

At breakfast, I told Sir Henry what I had seen. We decided to watch together for Barrymore that very night. Then Sir Henry got ready to go out. I got my hat and coat also.

Sir Henry looked at me. "What, Watson? Are you coming, too?" he asked.

"You know that Holmes has insisted I must not leave you alone," I reminded him.

Sir Henry said, "My dear fellow, I'm sure Holmes

could not guess what happened since I came here. Do you understand me? I must go out alone."

I did not know what to say or do. When he left, I began to worry that something terrible would happen to him. I set out after him at once in the direction of Merripit House.

I hurried along the road until I came to the top of a hill. There, about a quarter of a mile away, I could see Sir Henry and Miss Stapleton, deep in conversation. Then he put his arm around her, and it seemed as if she was pulling away from him.

Suddenly, they sprang apart. Stapleton was running wildly toward them! He was waving his arms dramatically, and, it seemed, yelling at Sir Henry. Then he turned on his heel and walked off, his sister following along behind him.

Sir Henry turned back toward home, the very picture of sorrow. I ran down the hill and met him. At first his eyes blazed when he learned that I had followed him. But then he laughed. "It seems the whole country has been out to see me," he said. "I don't understand it, Watson. From the first, I felt she was made for me. And she was happy too, I swear. But she wouldn't let me talk about love. She kept telling me this was a place of danger, and I ought to leave. Just now I told her that I wanted to marry her. But before she could answer, her brother came running up, screaming like a madman. He asked what I was doing with his sister. Did I think that just because I had a title I could do what I liked? Then he went off with her. I'm badly puzzled, Watson."

I was quite perplexed myself—but the next day, the matter was cleared up. Stapleton made a handsome apology. He explained that his sister is everything in his life. When he realized she might be taken away from him, it gave him a terrible shock. He was very sorry for what he had done. To make up for it, he invited us to dine at Merripit House next Friday.

Now I move on to the matter of the Barrymores. Congratulate me, Holmes—for this is one thread I have managed to remove from the tangled web.

As we had planned, Sir Henry and I sat up waiting for Barrymore. On the first night, we waited until nearly three o'clock. But on the next night, we soon heard footsteps in the hallway. When we followed Barrymore, we saw him watching out the window once again.

Sir Henry confronted him. "What are you doing

here, Barrymore?" he demanded.

The butler sprang back from the window, his eyes full of horror. "Don't ask me, sir!" he cried. "I give you my word that it is not *my* secret to tell!"

A sudden idea came to me. Taking the candle from Barrymore's shaking hand, I held it to the window. Out on the moor I could see a pinpoint of light shining in answer.

"*Look there!*" I cried.

Sir Henry turned to Barrymore. "You rascal! It seems you are in some dark plot against me!"

"Oh, no, sir, no!" a voice cried out. It was Mrs. Barrymore. "This is *my* doing, Sir Henry. My poor brother is out there on the moor—starving. Our light is a signal to show that food is ready for him. His light shows us the spot to bring it."

"Then your brother is . . ."

"The escaped convict, sir. I suppose we gave him his way too much when he was a boy. Somehow he came to think the world was made for his pleasure. When he grew older he met wicked friends. The devil entered into him until he broke my mother's heart and dragged our name in the dirt. But to me, sir, he was always the curly-headed little boy I took care of. When he dragged himself here, I could not bear to turn him away."

Sir Henry said, "Is this true, Barrymore?"

"Every word, Sir Henry."

"Go to bed now," said Sir Henry. "We will talk about this matter in the morning."

When they were gone, we stared at the tiny point of light out on the moor. Sir Henry said, "By thunder, Watson, I am going out to take that man!"

Five minutes later we were out on the moor. The clouds drove over the face of the sky. Now and again the moon peeped out for an instant. The tiny signal light still burned in the distance.

Suddenly we heard the howl, which rose and then fell in a deep moan. Again and again it sounded, filling the air over the moor.

"Watson," said Sir Henry, "that was the cry of a *hound*! Can there be truth in all these stories? I don't think I am a coward—but that sound seemed to freeze my very blood. Feel my hand!"

It was as cold as marble. "Shall we turn back?" I asked uncertainly.

"No, by thunder! We'll go after the convict, hell-hound or no."

We stumbled along in the darkness until we were very close. Finally, we saw the candle stuck in the middle of a tall rock. Then suddenly, a terrible animal face arose just ahead, its small eyes peering fiercely through the darkness.

We sprang forward. At that same moment, the convict screamed out a curse and threw a stone, which crashed close to our feet. Then he turned and ran, springing over the stones like a mountain goat. A lucky shot from my revolver might have crippled him. But I had brought it only to defend myself, not to shoot an unarmed man.

Sir Henry and I are both swift runners—but we had no chance of catching him. Finally, we stopped, panting hard.

It was at this moment the strangest thing happened. On a hill in the distance, lit by the moon, I saw the figure of a man. He seemed to be tall and thin. With a cry of surprise I turned to Sir Henry, but in that instant the figure disappeared.

"It must be one of the prison guards," said Sir Henry. "The moor has been thick with them since Selden escaped."

Well, perhaps this is true—but I should like to have more proof. While I believe I am making some progress in this case, it would be best if *you* could come as soon as you can.

8 A Clue from the Ashes

So far I have been able to quote from my reports to Sherlock Holmes. Now, however, I shall use pages from my diary to tell the story.

October 16th. A dull and foggy day with a drizzle of rain. I must say that the strange events of the last few days have shaken me. I feel a dread of dangerous times ahead.

We had a small scene after breakfast. Barrymore was upset that we went out after Selden.

"But the man is a *danger*!" insisted Sir Henry.

"He'll never trouble anyone in England again," said Barrymore. "Plans have been made for him to go to South America in a very few days. For God's sake, sir—I beg of you not to tell the police!"

"If he were safely out of the country," I said, "it would save the taxpayers quite a lot."

"That is true," said Sir Henry. "Well, Barrymore, perhaps if . . ."

"Thank you, sir, from the bottom of my heart!" cried Barrymore. "You've been so kind to us that I should like to do something for you in return. I know something about Sir Charles' death."

Sir Henry and I both jumped to our feet.

"I know why Sir Charles was waiting at the gate that night," Barrymore said. "It was to meet a woman."

"A *woman*? What was her name?" I asked.

"I do not know, sir," said Barrymore, "but her initials were L.L. Sir Charles had received a letter from Coombe Tracy that morning. I know because I found it later while I was cleaning out the fireplace. Most of the letter had been burned away, but we could read one bit at the end of the page. It said *Please, please, as you are a gentleman, burn this letter and meet me at the gate by ten o'clock.* It was signed L.L."

"We've said nothing about it," Barrymore went on. "To rake this up couldn't help our poor master."

"You thought it might hurt his reputation?"

"Well, sir, I thought no good could come of it."

"Very good, Barrymore. You can go." When the butler left, Sir Henry turned to me. "Well, Watson, what do you think of this new light?"

"It seems to leave the darkness blacker than before," I said. I decided to report the matter to Holmes at once. He must be busy indeed with his case in London, for his recent notes were few and short. I wished that he were here.

October 17th. The next day, I happened to meet Dr. Mortimer on a walk. He told me about a woman named Laura Lyons who lives in Coombe Tracy. He said that she is Frankland's daughter.

"She married an artist named Lyons," said Mortimer. "He turned out to be a rascal and deserted her. Since she had married without her father's consent, Frankland would have nothing to do with her. So, between the old man and the young one, the girl has had a pretty bad time."

"How does she live?" I asked.

"I imagine Frankland gives her a little," Dr. Mortimer said. "And fearing that she would go bad on her own, several of us gave her money to set up a typewriting business."

Mortimer was very curious about my interest in Mrs. Lyons. To divert him, I asked about his studies, and he willingly changed the subject. I have not lived for years with Sherlock Holmes for nothing.

Later that evening, I asked Barrymore if he had

heard any recent news of Selden.

"No, sir," said Barrymore. "Only that he took the food I left three days ago. That is, unless the other man took it."

I stared at Barrymore. "The *other* man? You've seen him, then?"

"No, sir—but Selden has. He lives in one of the stone huts. He has a boy working for him who brings him all he needs."

When Barrymore had gone, I stared out at the wet and windy moor. Tomorrow I shall do all a man can do to reach the heart of the mystery.

* * *

The pages from my diary have brought me up to the present. The events of the next few days are fixed in my memory.

On the nineteenth of October I went to see Laura Lyons. At first sight she seemed very beautiful. She had rich hazel eyes and dark hair, and a lovely bloom of pink on her cheeks. But as I looked at her more closely, there seemed something coarse about her.

"I have come to see you about Sir Charles," I explained.

"What can I tell you about him?" she asked. Her

fingers played nervously over her typewriter keys.

"You wrote to Sir Charles, did you not?" I asked.

She frowned. "What is the object of such a question?" she asked sharply.

"The object is to avoid a scandal. If you answer me now, the matter can stay out of the hands of the police."

Mrs. Lyons flushed with anger. "Yes," she said, "I did write him. Sir Charles was very kind to me. I wrote asking him for help."

"What sort of help?"

"Freedom from a husband that I hate. Every day I face the possibility that he might force me to live with him. But not long ago I learned that I could divorce him if I had enough money. That is why I wrote to Sir Charles."

"Did you ever plan to meet him?"

"*Really*, sir! Certainly not!"

"Surely your memory is wrong," I prompted her. "Your letter said, *as you are a gentleman, burn this letter, and be at the gate at ten o'clock.*"

Her face went deathly pale. She gasped in anger, "Is there no such thing as a gentleman?"

"Sir Charles *did* burn the letter—but parts of it could still be read. Tell me what happened when you met with him."

"Why, I never went," she said. "I swear to you. Something kept me from going. Anyway—it was a private matter."

Again and again I questioned her, but I could never get past that point. Finally, I left her and turned to that other clue. Who might I find in the stone huts of the moor?

For once, luck was with me. It came in the form of Mr. Frankland, whom I met on the road outside his house. He was in a fine mood.

"I don't know exactly where that convict is," he said, "but I think I can help the police lay their hands on him. I have seen with my own eyes the messenger who brings him food."

My heart sank for Barrymore. But then Frankland went on. "It's a child! I see him every day through my telescope on the roof. But wait, Dr. Watson! I think I see something moving on that hillside right now!"

We rushed upstairs to the telescope. "Quick, Watson!" he cried.

Sure enough, a small boy with a bundle was just passing over the top of the hill.

As soon as I could politely leave, I said goodbye to Frankland and hurried toward the hillside. Beyond the hill was a circle of stone huts. Only one of them still had something of a roof. Quietly, I walked up to it, my revolver in my hand. But when I looked inside, I saw that it was empty.

There were signs, however, that I had not followed a false scent. Inside were blankets and empty food cans. I also found a sheet of paper with a note that said, *Dr. Watson is in Coombe Tracy.*

It was *I*, then, and not Sir Henry, who was being followed. But by whom? I swore I would not leave the hut until I knew.

I waited. Outside, the sun was sinking. At last I heard the sound of boots on the stone outside. "It is a lovely evening, my dear Watson," said a familiar voice. "I really think you will be more comfortable outside."

9 A Dead Man on the Moor

A crushing weight of responsibility was suddenly lifted from my soul.

"*Holmes!*" I cried out gratefully.

"Come out," said he, "and please be careful with your revolver."

I stepped outside and grasped his hand.

"How did you find me?" he asked. "Did you spot me that night you chased the convict? I was careless enough to stand with my back to the moor."

"Yes, I saw you then."

"You must also have seen the boy through the old gentleman's telescope. I did not know what it was until I saw the light flashing upon the lens."

He rose and peered into the hut. "Ha!" he cried. "I see Cartwright has brought supplies. You remember Cartwright, the boy from the district office." He picked up the note. "And I see you have been to Coombe Tracy! To see Mrs. Laura Lyons?"

"Exactly."

"Well done!" said Holmes.

"But how in the name of wonder did you come here?" I asked, perplexed. "I thought you were busy with a case in London."

"That was what I wished you to think."

"You *used* me, yet you do not trust me!" I cried. "I think I deserve better at your hands, Holmes."

"My dear fellow, you have been an invaluable help. But I could not get around easily if people knew I was here."

"But why keep *me* in the dark?"

"If you had known I was here, you might have wished to tell me something, or come here to bring me something. It was simply too risky."

"My reports have been wasted!" I grunted.

Holmes took a bundle of papers from his pocket. "Here are your reports, which I have read several times. I had them sent from London. You have shown great intelligence in this difficult case."

In the warmth of Holmes' praise, my anger disappeared. When he asked me to describe the meeting with Laura Lyons, I promptly obliged him.

"Did you know that Stapleton and Laura Lyons are very close?" Holmes asked.

"No, I did not."

"This puts a powerful weapon into our hands," Holmes said. "Now, if I could use it to bring his wife to our side . . ."

"His *wife?*"

"Yes," said Holmes. "The lady Stapleton calls his sister is actually his wife."

"But why . . ."

"Because she is much more useful to Stapleton if she pretends to be a free woman."

"How could Stapleton have let Sir Henry fall in love with her?" I sputtered.

"He knew that could hurt no one but Sir Henry," Holmes explained patiently.

"Then *Stapleton* is our enemy? He's the one who followed us in London?"

"Yes."

"And the warning message must have come from Stapleton's wife?"

"Exactly," said Holmes. "Stapleton made a mistake when he told you his story. The school he owned actually existed. When it closed, the records say that he disappeared with his wife."

"Where does Laura Lyons come in?" I asked.

"Since she believes Stapleton to be a single man,

she is counting on him to marry her," said Holmes.

"When should she learn the truth?" I asked.

"Tomorrow. It must be our first duty to visit her. But it is getting dark now, Watson. Don't you think you should be getting back to Sir Henry?"

"One last question, Holmes," I said as I rose. "What is Stapleton after?"

Holmes' voice sank. "It is murder," he said, "cold-blooded murder. But do not ask me for details. My nets are closing in on him, just as his are closing in on Sir Henry. The only danger is if he strikes before we are ready. *Listen!*"

A terrible scream and then a loud cry of horror and pain broke the silence of the moor.

Then came a long, low howl.

"The *hound*!" cried Holmes. "Come, Watson! Good heavens! If we are too late . . ."

Blindly, we ran through the dark, panting our way up hills and forcing ourselves through bushes. To the left, we heard a low moan. There, at the bottom of a jagged cliff, a man lay face down on the ground. His head was doubled up under him at a horrible angle. I realized that the moan we had heard must have been the passing of his soul.

When Holmes lit a match, I saw the man's tweed

suit—it was Sir Henry Baskerville!

"The *brute*!" I cried. "I can never forgive myself for leaving him alone tonight!"

"I am more to blame than you," Holmes muttered to himself. "Fool that I was to wait! In order to have my case complete, I have thrown away his life. This is the greatest mistake of my career!"

"Stapleton shall pay for this!" I cried.

"He shall," said Holmes. "But we have yet to prove the link between the man and the beast. We cannot swear that Sir Henry was killed by the hound. It is clear he died from a fall."

Holmes bent over the body. Then suddenly, he began laughing and dancing and wringing my hand.

"It is the *convict*!" he cried.

We turned the body over and I saw the savage face of Selden! In an instant, it was all clear to me. Sir Henry had given his old clothes to Barrymore. The butler had passed on this suit to Selden for his escape from the country. The tragedy was still black enough—but Selden had deserved death by the laws of his own country.

"It is clear the hound has followed the scent of Sir Henry's clothes," Holmes said, "probably the boot that was taken from his hotel. But why was the hound set loose tonight? Surely Stapleton would not let it out unless he knew that Sir Henry was on the moor."

We decided to leave the body in one of the huts until we could send for the police. Just then Holmes saw Stapleton coming toward us.

"Why, Dr. Watson, that's not *you*, is it?" Stapleton called. "You're the last man I thought I would be seeing out on the moor so late. But, dear me, what's this? Is somebody hurt? No—don't tell me that is our friend Sir Henry?"

He rushed past me and bent over the body. I heard him gasp.

"Who—who's *this*?" he cried.

"It's Selden, the escaped convict."

Stapleton's face was white. With a great effort, he hid his surprise and disappointment. He looked sharply from Holmes to me.

"He seems to have broken his neck from a fall," I said. "My friend and I were out walking when we heard him cry out."

"I heard a cry also," Stapleton said. "I was worried about Sir Henry."

I asked, "Why Sir Henry?"

"Because I had suggested that he come for a visit. When he hadn't arrived, I became worried. By the way, did you hear any strange sound besides the cry?"

"No," said Holmes. "What do you mean?"

"Oh, you know the stories people tell about the hound," said Stapleton. "But tell me. What do *you* think of all this, Mr. Sherlock Holmes?"

"You are quick to recognize me," Holmes said.

"We have been expecting you for some time," said Stapleton. "Perhaps you can explain some of the strange events that have happened here."

"Unfortunately, I will be returning to London tomorrow," said Holmes. "A detective needs facts—not stories and legends. I'm afraid this has been a disappointing case."

We said goodnight and walked back to Baskerville Hall, while Stapleton continued on alone. The moon shone silver on the spot where Selden had come to his terrible end.

§10 Ambush at Grimpen Mire

As Holmes and I walked back toward Baskerville Hall, I asked, "Why not arrest Stapleton at once?"

"My dear Watson," said Holmes. "You were born a man of action! But as yet we can prove nothing against him. Sir Charles' body was found without a mark on it—and a hound does not bite a dead body. No, Sir Charles was dead before the hound reached him. Even tonight we had no real link between the hound and the man's death."

Sir Henry welcomed us at the hall. Before supper, I told the Barrymores the news of Selden's death. Barrymore looked relieved, but his wife cried bitterly into her apron. To her, Selden would always be the little boy she remembered from her girlhood.

Over supper, Sir Henry asked Holmes about the case. Holmes said, "I think the chances are good that it will soon be solved. I have no doubt—"

Then he stopped suddenly and stared at something over my head. "Excuse me," he said, "that is really a very fine portrait of the gentleman in black velvet and lace."

"Ah," said Sir Henry. "I'm afraid he is the cause of all this trouble—the wicked Sir Hugo."

"Dear me," said Holmes. "He seems a quiet-looking man. I pictured him more rough-looking."

During supper, Holmes said little. But when Sir Henry had gone to bed, he led me back to the portrait. "Do you see anything there?" he asked.

I looked intently at the stern mouth and the cold eyes of Sir Hugo and shook my head.

Then Holmes curved his arm in front of the portrait, hiding the broad hat and long, curly hair.

"Good heavens!" I cried.

I was astounded. The face of *Stapleton* had sprung out of the picture.

"Ha!" said Holmes. "The fellow is a Baskerville, beyond a doubt. *We have him*, Watson!"

Holmes burst out laughing. I have not often heard him laugh, and it has always meant bad luck to somebody.

The next morning, Sir Henry greeted Holmes. "Good morning! I must say that you look like a general planning his battle strategy."

"That is the exact situation," said Holmes.

"Then I need my orders," said Sir Henry.

"Very good," said Holmes. "I understand you are having supper with the Stapletons tonight. Unfortunately, Watson and I cannot join you. We must return to London."

I could see Sir Henry was hurt by our leaving him alone. "Very well," he said coldly.

"One more thing," said Holmes. "When you return from Merripit House tonight, you must walk home."

"But that is the very thing you have warned me *not* to do."

"This time you may do it with safety," Holmes said. "You must trust me."

"I will do just as you say," said Sir Henry.

A few hours later we were at the train station at Coombe Tracy. Cartwright was there to meet us with a telegram. It read:

> *Received your wire. Coming down with warrant. Arrive 5:40.*
> *LESTRADE.*

Holmes said, "Lestrade is the finest of the

professional detectives, I think, and we may need his help. Now, Watson, I think the best way to spend our time would be to visit Mrs. Laura Lyons."

Mrs. Lyons was in her office. Holmes came straight to the point. "I am investigating the case of Sir Charles' death," he said. "We believe Sir Charles was murdered. The evidence points not only to your friend Mr. Stapleton, but to his wife as well."

The lady sprang from her chair. "His *wife?*" she cried out in hurt and anger. "Prove it to me!"

Holmes drew a photograph from his pocket. "As you see, the picture is labeled *Mr. and Mrs. Vandeleur,* but you will have no trouble recognizing this man and woman."

She looked at the photograph and then at us. "Mr. Holmes, this man had offered me marriage. He has lied to me—the villain—in every way! Now I see that I was nothing but a tool in his hands. I will tell you all I know."

"Then it was Stapleton who had you write the letter to Sir Charles?" asked Holmes.

"Yes," she admitted.

"And after the letter had been sent, it was he who told you not to keep the appointment with

Sir Charles at the gate to the moor?"

"He told me it would hurt his self-respect. He said he would give every last penny he had to help me divorce my husband."

"When news of Sir Charles' death came out, did Stapleton make you swear to tell nothing about your appointment?"

"Yes, he said that *I* would be suspected if the facts came out."

"You had Stapleton in your power and yet you are alive," said Holmes. "I think you have had a lucky escape, Mrs. Lyons."

We went back to the train station to meet the express from London. A small bulldog of a man stepped out to greet us. "Anything good?" he asked.

"The biggest thing in years, Lestrade," said Holmes as he shook the man's hand.

We hired a wagon to take us part of the way to Merripit House. Then we paid the driver and set off on foot. It was a gloomy night. A huge lake of fog hovered over the Grimpen Mire.

When we were about 200 yards from Merripit House, Holmes told us to stop. "We shall make our little ambush here," he said. "Watson, creep up to the house and see what they are doing."

I tiptoed down the path and peered into the window. Only Sir Henry and Stapleton were in the room. Sir Henry looked pale. Perhaps the thought of the lonely walk home was on his mind.

I returned to Holmes and Lestrade. Like a thick wall, the fog was closing in. Holmes was worried. "This is the one thing on earth that could spoil my plans," he said. "Sir Henry can't stay much longer. It is already ten o'clock. His very life could depend on his coming out before the fog blots out the path."

With every minute, the white fog drifted closer. We crept as close to the house as we dared.

At last we heard the sound of Sir Henry's steps as he made his way through the fog.

"Look out!" said Holmes as he cocked his pistol. "It's coming!"

The Hound Attacks

I heard something running through the fog. Then, suddenly, Lestrade gave a yell of terror and threw himself on the ground. Out of the fog sprang an enormous, coal-black hound—but such a hound as no creature on earth has seen! Tongues of fire burst from its open mouth. Its jaws appeared to be lined with red, flickering sparks.

As the beast went leaping past us, Holmes and I both fired at once. The thing gave a terrible howl.

Sir Henry screamed. As I ran toward him, I watched the beast throw him to the ground and dive at his throat. But in the next instant, Holmes had emptied his revolver into the beast's side. With a last howl of pain, it fell to the ground.

We ran to where Sir Henry lay and tore away his collar. Holmes breathed a prayer of thanks. There was no wound. Sir Henry opened his eyes. "What was it?" he whispered hoarsely.

"It's dead, whatever it is," said Holmes.

The hound was the size of a small lioness. Even now, its mouth seemed to drip with a bluish flame. I placed my hand on the glowing jaw. My own fingers shone faintly in the darkness.

"*Phosphorus!*" I cried in amazement.

Holmes turned to Sir Henry. "We owe you a deep apology for giving you such a fright. I was prepared for a hound—but nothing like this."

"You saved my life!"

"After first putting you in danger," said Holmes, apologetically. "We must leave you now. The rest of our work must be done—and quickly!"

At Merripit House, we found Mrs. Stapleton wrapped in sheets and tied to a post.

"Is he safe?" she asked.

"He cannot escape us, madam."

"No, no, I did not mean my husband. Is Sir Henry safe? And what of the hound?"

"Sir Henry is safe and the hound is dead."

She gave a sigh of relief. "Thank God! See how this villain has treated me!" She held out her arms, which were covered with bruises. "But this is nothing! It hurts even more to see I have been only his tool." She broke into sobs.

"If you have ever helped him in evil," said Holmes, "erase your sin by leading us to him."

"There is only one place he could be," she said. "The old tin mine—in the heart of Grimpen Mire."

It was useless to hunt for Stapleton until the fog had lifted. We left Lestrade at the house and went back to Baskerville Hall. The truth about Beryl Stapleton could no longer be kept from Sir Henry, but he took the news bravely. The shock of the night's adventures, however, had badly shattered his nerves. It would be many months before Sir Henry would fully recover.

The next morning, Mrs. Stapleton led us over the path through the Grimpen Mire. Along the way, something caught Holmes' eye. He stepped off the path and sank to his waist in the ooze. He lifted an old black boot in the air.

"Sir Henry's missing boot," cried Holmes. "At least Stapleton came this far."

But no other sign of Stapleton could be found. Somewhere in the heart of the great Grimpen Mire that cold and cruel-hearted man is buried forever.

# A Scent of Jasmine

One raw and foggy night in November, Holmes and I sat before a blazing fire. It was then that Holmes cleared up the last puzzling details of the Baskerville case.

"After a few long talks with Mrs. Stapleton," Holmes began, "I learned more of her story. Stapleton was indeed a Baskerville. He was the son of Rodger Baskerville—the younger brother of Sir Charles, who went to South America. It was thought that he had died unmarried, but, in fact, he had a son. The boy was also named Rodger.

"Rodger married Beryl Garcia, one of the beauties of Costa Rica. After stealing a large sum of money, he changed his name to Vandeleur. Then he came to England and started a school.

"It was after the school closed that he changed his name to Stapleton. Around this time he also discovered that *two* lives stood between him and his inheritance of a valuable estate.

"He became friends with Sir Charles. He learned the old man had a weak heart and that he took the legend of the hound quite seriously. The task was to lure Sir Charles from his house at night. He tried to use his wife to do this, but she refused, even though he hit her. It was then that he turned to Mrs. Laura Lyons, who made the fatal appointment.

"That night, Stapleton painted the dog with phosphorus and let him loose. The sight of the beast was too much for Sir Charles' weak heart.

"Rodger's next step was to rid himself of Sir Henry. I am sure he bribed a maid to steal some of his clothing. The first boot they stole, of course, was useless because it was new. It did not yet have Sir Henry's scent. That is why a second boot was taken. When the boots were stolen, I knew we must be dealing with a *real* hound.

"I also knew that a woman had sent Sir Henry the warning note. There was a scent of jasmine perfume on the paper. Of course, she did not dare to warn Sir Henry in person. She was much too afraid of Stapleton's anger."

"On the night of the crisis, she suspected that Stapleton meant to harm Sir Henry. She accused him, and they fought. It was then that she found out about Mrs. Lyons. Her loyalty to Stapleton instantly turned to hate. He tied her up so she would have no chance to warn Sir Henry. Now he was free to use the hound for murder."

"Just one more question, Holmes," I said. "Once Sir Henry was dead, how would Rodger be able to claim the Baskerville fortune? After all, everyone knew him as *Stapleton*."

"Mrs. Stapleton heard her husband puzzling over the problem," Holmes explained. "He said he could move to South America and claim the money from there. Or he could disguise himself. He could also have hired another man to play the part. I am sure he would have come up with a clever plan.

"And now, Watson, we have had some weeks of difficult work. For one evening, I think we may turn our thoughts to more pleasant subjects. I have a box for the theatre. Can you be ready in half an hour? We can stop at Marcini's for a little dinner on the way."